FRIENDS FOREVER?

by Diana G. Gallagher

illustrated by Brann Garvey

Librarian Reviewer
Laurie K. Holland
Media Specialist (National Board Certified), Edina, MN
MA in Elementary Education, Minnesota State University, Mankato

Reading Consultant
Sherry Klehr
Elementary/Middle School Educator, Edina Public Schools, MN
MA in Education, University of Minnesota

Claudia Cristina Cortez is published by Stone Arch Books
151 Good Counsel Drive, P.O. Box 669
Mankato, Minnesota 56002
www.stonearchbooks.com

Library of Congress Cataloging-in-Publication Data
Gallagher, Diana G.
    Friends Forever?: The Complicated Life of Claudia Cristina Cortez / by
Diana G. Gallagher; illustrated by Brann Garvey.
    p. cm. — (Claudia Cristina Cortez)
    ISBN 978-1-4342-0772-2 (library binding)
    ISBN 978-1-4342-0868-2 (pbk.)
    [1. Cheerleading—Fiction. 2. Conduct of life—Fiction. 3. Middle
schools—Fiction. 4. Schools—Fiction.] I. Garvey, Brann, ill. II. Title.
PZ7.G13543Fri 2009
[Fic]—dc21   2008004285

Summary: The cheerleaders are chosen unfairly, but Monica wants to try out
anyway. How can Claudia support her and change the way things work at school?

Art Director: Heather Kindseth
Graphic Designer: Kay Fraser

Photo Credits
Delaney Photography, cover, 1

1 2 3 4 5 6 13 12 11 10 09 08

Printed in the United States of America

Table of Contents

Cast of

CLAUDIA

That's me. I'm thirteen, and I'm in the seventh grade at Pine Tree Middle School. I live with my mom, my dad, and my brother, Jimmy. I have one cat, Ping-Ping. I like music, baseball, and hanging out with my friends.

ME

MONICA is my very best friend. We met when we were really little, and we've been best friends ever since. I don't know what I'd do without her! Monica loves horses. In fact, when she grows up, she wants to be an Olympic rider!

MONICA

BECCA is one of my closest friends. She lives next door to Monica. Becca is really, really smart. She gets good grades. She's also really good at art.

BECCA

ADAM and I met when we were in third grade. Now that we're teenagers, we don't spend as much time together as we did when we were kids, but he's always there for me when I need him. (Plus, he's the only person who wants to talk about baseball with me!)

ADAM

Characters

TOMMY's our class clown. Sometimes he's really funny, but sometimes he is just annoying. Becca has a crush on him . . . but I'd never tell.

I think **PETER** is probably the smartest person I've ever met. Seriously. He's even smarter than our teachers! He's also one of my friends. Which is lucky, because sometimes he helps me with homework.

Every school has a bully, and **JENNY** is ours. She's the tallest person in our class, and the meanest, too. She always threatens to stomp people. No one's ever seen her stomp anyone, but that doesn't mean it hasn't happened!

ANNA is the most popular girl at our school. Everyone wants to be friends with her. I think that's weird, because Anna can be really, really mean. I mostly try to stay away from her.

Cast of

CARLY

CARLY is Anna's best friend. She always tries to act exactly like Anna does. She even wears the exact same clothes. She's never really been mean to me, but she's never been nice to me either!

NICK

NICK is my annoying seven-year-old neighbor. I get stuck babysitting him a lot. He likes to make me miserable. (Okay, he's not that bad ALL of the time . . . just most of the time.)

BRAD

BRAD is our school's football star. He's really popular, really nice, and really cute. Only Becca and Monica know that I have a really big crush on him! I usually feel too embarrassed to talk to him, unless I really, really have to.

Characters

KAREN is one of Anna's friends. So of course she's trying out for the cheerleading squad.

KAREN

GINA

GINA is in eighth grade. She's also the captain of the cheerleading squad. She gets to pick the people who will make the team. I don't know her well, but she doesn't seem very nice!

KRISTIN is really good at math. She's one of the girls who's trying out for the cheerleading squad.

KRISTIN

CHAPTER 1

Leadership Lesson

English is my **favorite** class. History is my **second favorite** subject. Sometimes, Ms. Stark tells us an **interesting** story in history class.

It is sort of like English class, **but the stories are true.** People wrote down what happened in the past, or they drew pictures.

So history class is like *a time machine that only goes backward.* I think that's cool.

Ms. Stark doesn't tell an interesting story in history every day. Today, we talked about **leadership.**

"A leader guides or leads a group or activity," Ms. Stark explained. "Can anyone give me an example?"

"*Follow the leader,*" Brad Turino said. "The kids game."

No one giggled, even though Brad was talking about **kid stuff.** No one wanted to **embarrass** the captain of the football team.

He's also GORGEOUS and NICE. And he must be a good leader, because I'd follow him anywhere.

I've had a **secret crush** on Brad for years. Only Monica and Becca know about it. They're two of my **best friends.** My other best friend is Adam, but since he's a BOY, I don't tell him everything.

"Good, Brad," Ms. Stark said. "Anyone else?" Tommy jiggled in his seat and waved. He was the class clown. I couldn't tell if he wanted to answer Ms. Stark's question or go to the bathroom.

"Yes, Tommy?" Ms. Stark asked.

Tommy jumped up. He put his hands by his head and wiggled his fingers. Then he bugged out his eyes. **"Take me to your leader! Or else!"** he yelled in a weird alien voice.

Becca tried not to laugh. She has a secret crush on Tommy.

Jenny Pinski groaned. "Rotten joke, Tommy."

Jenny doesn't like anyone. We don't care. We just stay out of her way. She's wanted to stomp someone since kindergarten.

"How rotten was it?" Tommy asked.

Jenny held her nose.

Tommy sighed and sat down.

"Anyone else?" Ms. Stark asked.

Carly raised her hand. I was sort of surprised.
Carly isn't stupid. She just doesn't care about
grades. She forgets facts unless the topic is clothes
or Pine Tree Middle School **gossip.** So if Carly knows
an answer, it's **a big deal.**

"The leader of the band!" she said.

Jenny groaned again.

"Can anyone name a person who's an
example of a good leader?" Ms. Stark asked.

"Sam Willie, the lead guitar player in my
favorite band, **Bad Dog**," **Sylvia** answered.

Then Anna raised her hand. "Me!" **Anna**
exclaimed. "I'm a leader because everyone
wants to be friends with me."

Ms. Stark smiled. "I meant someone from the
past," she explained.

"President Abraham Lincoln!" **Peter** shouted out. He's a SUPER BRAIN and a little shy. When everyone looked at him, he slid down in his seat.

"That's an excellent example," Ms. Stark said. "Why was **Abraham Lincoln** a good leader?"

Nobody answered.

So Ms. Stark told us about being a good leader. I took notes.

A Great Leader

1. Does the right thing even if others don't like it.

2. Inspires others to do the right thing.

3. Is not afraid to fail.

I wanted to be a great leader.

CHAPTER 2

Follow Up

Monica, Becca, and I had lunch right after history class. We walked to the cafeteria together.

"Claudia is a **natural leader**," Becca said.

"I am?" I asked, surprised.

Becca nodded. "You think up **crazy things** to do," she explained. "And Monica always goes along with your ideas."

Monica frowned. "No, I don't," she said.

"Yes, you do," Becca said. "Even when you might get into trouble."

That happens a lot. The 𝒯𝑅𝒪𝒰𝐵𝐿𝐸 part, I mean.

Some of My Crazy Ideas and the Terrible Consequences

Crazy Idea #1: Gave my Siamese cat a bath with the hose.

Terrible Consequence #1: Ping–Ping freaked out. She turned into a yowling, spitting bundle of soggy fur with claws. Monica and I got scratched, and Ping-Ping wouldn't let me pet her for a week.

Crazy Idea #2: Told **Nick** he'd get hives if he ate our dried apricots. He ate our dried apricots. Then Monica and I told him to put butter on his arms so he wouldn't get hives.

Terrible Consequence #2: Nick is a brat, but he's only seven, so he believed us. He buttered his arms, hugged his mom, and ruined her favorite silk shirt. We were grounded for a week.

Crazy Idea #3: Ordered 10 "free" magazines on the Internet.

Terrible Consequence #3: I didn't read the rules carefully. Only the first month was free. I got a bill for $263.00, and Monica's bill was even bigger! Dad told the magazine people Monica and I were kids.

We didn't have to pay for the magazines, but my dad and Monica's mom made us read the free magazines. *Even the boring parts. Even the ads. Every single word!*

I couldn't remember all the crazy ideas I ever had. The complete list was huge, but Monica always went along with them.

Becca didn't. If she thought we'd get into trouble, she headed home.

"I want to be a **great leader**," I said. "From now on I'll only think up good stuff that won't get us in trouble."

Becca smiled. "Works for me," she said.

"Not me," **Monica** said. "I'm not going to follow anyone anywhere anymore."

CHAPTER 3

Shocking News

After lunch, it was time for gym class. I loved gym class, but some girls didn't.

Some girls don't like gym because:

1. Gym clothes are kind of ugly.

2. Working out messes up your hair and makes you sweat.

3. Some girls aren't good at sports.

Girls who *aren't good at sports* usually *don't like sports*. Anna isn't good at sports, for example. So she always says she doesn't like sports.

Except one.

"There is room on the eighth-grade cheerleading squad for some seventh graders. The seventh-grade girls will have to try out. The tryouts will be held next week," said Ms. Campbell, our gym teacher.

Almost everyone cheered. Anna and Carly yelled happily and jumped for joy. **I wasn't excited. I didn't jump.**

"How many new girls does the squad need?" **Anna** asked sweetly. She smiled and bounced with **enthusiasm.**

Becca whispered, "What a FAKE!"

I nodded and rolled my eyes. Anna is not sweet or adorable. She's MEAN and SELFISH.

"She's trying to **impress** Ms. Campbell," I whispered back.

"Why?" **Becca** asked. "That won't help her get on the squad."

Ms. Campbell taught gym and coached some of the sports teams. But she didn't pick the new cheerleaders. **The eighth graders on the cheerleading squad were going to choose the new seventh graders.**

"Four girls left the team when they moved this year," Ms. Campbell said. "So we need four new seventh-grade girls to replace them."

Everyone CHEERED again. Except Becca and me.

"I've always wanted to be a cheerleader," **Carly** said.

"Me too," **Karen** said. She was another one of Anna's friends. "I just have to make the squad."

"Don't worry," Anna said. **"We will."** She spoke softly so Ms. Campbell wouldn't hear.

"I've never wanted to be a cheerleader," Becca said.

I already knew that. Monica, Becca, and I told each other everything. I knew their **deepest, darkest secrets,** and they knew mine. We never talked about cheerleading.

"Cheerleaders are *conceited*," Becca continued. "Just like **Anna** and her friends."

I was **impulsive** and **curious,** and I talked too much. Sometimes Becca was so **careful** that she wasn't any fun. Monica didn't always 𝒯𝐻𝐼𝒩𝒦 before she did things. Like going along with my 𝒞𝑅𝒜𝒵𝒴 ideas. But we're not stuck up.

"I'm going to try out," Monica said.

Becca and I gasped. We were both **shocked speechless.** Monica couldn't have said anything that shocked me more — even if she had said she wanted to **train elephants to rollerskate.**

CHAPTER 4

Discouraging Words

Becca and I walked home with Monica. We tried to change her mind about being a cheerleader.

A Real Friend

. . . tells a friend when she's making a mistake.

"Cheerleading is **hard work,**" I told Monica. "You'll have to practice for tryouts every day."

"And practice harder for the games," Becca said.

"If you make the squad," I added.

"I don't mind hard work," **Monica** said.

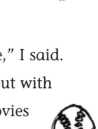

She was right about that. There was no way that I could accuse Monica of being LAZY. I tried something else.

"Cheerleading takes up too much time," I said. "If I were a cheerleader, I couldn't hang out with you guys or play baseball or go to the movies or watch Nick."

I stopped talking. My seven-year-old neighbor, **Nick**, was the **Menace of Market Street!** (That's where we lived.) It would've been great to not have to watch him!

"All the games are on Saturday," Becca reminded Monica.

"Right," I said. "You'll have to quit taking your horseback-riding lessons."

I thought that would get her. Horses were **#1** through **#10** on **Monica's Top Ten list of favorite things.** She absolutely loved horses. She collected glass horses and horse movies, and her bedroom walls were covered with posters of horses.

"I wouldn't give up my art lessons for anything," Becca said.

"I don't have to give up horseback riding," Monica said. "I can change my riding times. That's not a big deal."

I was STUNNED. Once, Monica missed Tommy's **birthday party** because she wouldn't cancel her riding lesson. She HATED missing lessons.

"Cheerleaders have to look PERFECT," Becca said. "Like fashion models."

"No flyaway hair allowed," I added. "You'll have to use your allowance to pay for hairspray."

"And you have to be PERKY!" Becca said. She held up her hands. Then she made a big, fake smile and waved her hands around.

I copied Becca's dorky dance. **"Happy, happy all the time,"** I squealed.

"If I'm picked to be a cheerleader, I will be happy," Monica said. "All the time." *She sounded kind of annoyed.*

I should have shut up, but I didn't. I kept talking.

"If Gina doesn't like you, *she won't pick you,*" I said.

Gina is the eighth-grade version of Anna. She's also the captain of the cheerleading squad.

"The **whole squad** gets to vote," Monica said.

"The other cheerleaders will do what Gina wants," Becca said.

"And being **popular** counts more than being good," I said.

"Anna, Carly, and Karen will make the squad for sure," Becca told Monica.

4 cheerleaders needed - 3 popular girls = 1 spot open

"So your chances probably aren't very good," I said. I wasn't trying to insult Monica. I was just being honest. *The cool kids always got picked.* That was just a **fact** of middle-school life.

"I'm going to try out anyway," Monica said.

"Why?" I asked. "I just don't get it."

"I want to do something cool," **Monica** explained. "And I want to be a leader. That's what cheerleaders are. They stand in front of big crowds and get them to cheer."

"That's not the kind of leader Ms. Stark meant," I said.

"You're just mad because I want to do something on my own," Monica muttered. **She glared at me.**

"I'm not mad," I said.

I didn't want to argue. I hated arguing with Monica. Once, in fourth grade, we had a big fight. We both wanted to take **the class rat** home for winter break. Our teacher settled the argument. She let someone else rat-sit Toby.

Monica and I didn't talk for two weeks. It was a horrible vacation. We made up the first day back at school. **And we promised not to fight about anything silly ever again.**

Three years later, we hadn't had a single fight since.

Monica didn't think cheerleading was silly.

I shut up.

CHAPTER 5

Good Ideas, No Takers

Great leaders fight for great causes.

I couldn't make a new country, like **George Washington** did.

Or start the **Red Cross** to help people, like Clara Barton did.

There just weren't any big causes for seventh graders. Not at Pine Tree Middle School, anyway.

So I decided to fight for *a little cause.*

"I have a great idea," I said at lunch the next day. "Let's put all the **wrappers** from our **straws** in the paper recycling bin instead of throwing them away."

"Why?" Adam asked. He ripped the end off his straw wrapper. Then he blew the wrapper right at Peter.

Peter ducked. The wrapper hit Tommy in the face.

"Wrapper war!" **Tommy** yelled. He aimed his straw at Peter.

Peter's wrapper hit Tommy first. "I win!" Peter yelled, smiling.

"Come on, guys," I said. "This is serious."

"What is?" Monica asked.

"Recycling straw wrappers," I explained. "The paper company can use old straw wrappers to make new ones. **We can save a tree.**"

Tommy wadded up his wrapper and threw it at Adam. He missed, and the wrapper landed on the floor.

Ms. Stark was watching. "Did you drop something, Tommy?" she asked, folding her arms.

"Oops!" Tommy said. He ran over to pick up the wrapper. He made a jump shot. The wrapper went into a **trashcan**. "Two points!" he yelled.

"Why didn't you put it in the recycle bin?" I asked.

"I *forgot*," Tommy said. He shrugged. "Sorry."

"**Recycling** is a good idea. Right, Peter?" I asked.

Peter was the *smartest* kid in the whole school. I was sure he'd agree with me.

Peter looked up. "Do you have an idea for a project?" he asked.

"What project?" I asked nervously. **My heart flip-flopped.** I felt panicky. "Do we have a project due? For what class?"

"Not for class. For the museum science fair," Peter explained. He sighed. "I can't decide. Should I make electricity with **wind, water,** or **solar power?**"

"You could recycle straw wrappers," I suggested. "That would **save energy,** wouldn't it?"

"I'll do wind, water, and sun," Peter said. "That might win first place."

I dropped my head on my arms. I was ANNOYED and **frustrated.** Nobody was listening to me. Not even Monica and Becca.

"I bet you're right, Becca," Monica said quietly. She stared at Anna's table. "Gina will pick Anna and her friends."

"Yep," **Becca** said.

"But only three of them are trying out," Monica said. "The team will still need **one more new girl.**" She looked at Becca. "Will you help me practice?"

"Nope," Becca said.

"Why not?" Monica asked. "I thought we were friends."

"We are," Becca said. "That's why I won't help you become **a snobby cool kid.** Besides, the cheerleaders at our school do the mean kind of cheers."

"What's a **mean cheer?**" Monica asked.

"One that makes fun of the other team," Becca explained. "Or **INSULTS** them. Like this."

Becca recited a basketball cheer.

"We're the best, and you're not.

Cougars never miss a shot.

You're okay, but we're way better.

Cougars win! We're go-go-getters!"

That gave me an idea. "Maybe you can STOP the mean cheers, Monica," I said.

"I'm not a cheerleader yet," Monica said. "And **Gina's** the captain."

"Gina's a bad leader," I explained. "A good leader would have fair tryouts, not a *popularity contest*. And she wouldn't do mean cheers."

"Yeah, but who would be a better leader?" Monica asked.

"You!" I exclaimed. "You want to be a leader. **This is your chance.**"

"I just want to make the squad," Monica said.

I sighed. Someone needed to stop the mean cheers. It was the right thing to do. But I couldn't make Monica lead if she didn't want to. I decided to help her practice anyway.

"Let's start training tomorrow," I said.

The bell rang, and we all stood up to leave.

"Don't forget to **recycle** your straw wrappers!" I called out.

Everyone was in a hurry. They all forgot.

How could I be a great leader? **I couldn't even get my friends to save a tree!**

CHAPTER 6

Training Tactics

Day 1

After school, Monica and I went to my house. We headed into the living room. Then we heard a SCREAM.

Nick ran in. He took a flying leap and then he belly-flopped onto the sofa.

"Does he have to be here?" Monica asked.

The answer to that question is always, "Yes."

1. Nick's mom goes somewhere almost every day.

2. My mom is a good neighbor.

3. Nick stays at our house.

4. Mom pays me $2.00 an hour to watch him.

5. I can't get out of it. (Not for any reason. Not even if I'm sick or have a ton of homework or chores or something really important to do like help my best friend become a cheerleader even if I don't think she should.)

Watching Nick wasn't easy. He didn't listen. He yelled. He was constantly lying. And he liked being bad. There was only one way to make him behave. **Bribery.**

"Sit still and be quiet, Nick," I said. "Then you can watch a DVD with us."

"What DVD?" Nick asked. *"Viper Man and the Doom Buggy? Space Rat Race?"*

Monica frowned. "I thought we were going to practice," she said.

"First we have to learn what to do," I said. "I got a cheerleading DVD at the library."

"Girl stuff! No way!" Nick yelled. He jumped up and down on the sofa. "I want to watch Viper Man!"

"Do you want some cookies and milk?" I asked.

Nick stopped jumping and asked, "Is it **chocolate milk?**"

"Sure," I said. "Whatever."

Nick sat down.

I got milk and cookies for everyone.

Then we watched the DVD. Monica and I took notes.

The DVD started with a cheer. Six girls shook their pom-poms. They smiled. They jumped and chanted with GUSTO.

Gusto means energy and enthusiasm. It's the perfect word for cheerleading. And Nick.

Nick waved his arms and yelled, "I can do that! **Two! Four! Six!"**

I stuffed a cookie in his mouth.

Day 2

The next day after school, I went to Monica's house. She was wearing a short white skirt. She even had pom-poms. "This is *my mom's old tennis outfit,*" Monica explained. "Dad gave me the pom-poms. I practiced using them last night."

"Great! Show me a cheer," I said.

Monica moved her arms up in a V. Then down in a V. Then into her chest and out to the side three times.

She finished with a hop. **It wasn't high enough to be a jump.**

She did the moves twice and chanted while she moved.

"Go Green! Go Gold!

Cougars, Cougars, fast and bold!

Go Gold! Go Green!

Go, Cougars! Go team!"

Monica stopped to catch her breath. "How was that?" she asked.

"Not bad," I lied.

Monica had done everything wrong.

1. Sloppy movements

2. Quiet words

3. Stiff shoulders

"But you want to be the 𝔅𝔈𝔖𝔗, right?" I added. I didn't want to hurt her feelings. I wanted to help her as much as I could.

"Right," Monica agreed.

"Good," I said, smiling. "You have to say the words clearly. And punch your arm and leg movements. Don't drag them."

"Like this?" Monica asked. She raised her arms. She moved one leg to the side and bent her knee. That move was called a **lunge.**

"Better," I lied again. It didn't look at all like the lunges we'd seen on the DVD. "Try moving your arms and legs at the same time," I suggested.

Monica lunged again. That time, she almost had it.

"Yeah!" I shouted. "That was great. Did you do the exercises on the DVD? That will make your muscles stronger."

"I'd rather do the fun stuff," Monica said. She tried a split jump. It's called a **spread eagle.** She fell down when she landed, so it was more like a **turkey tumble.**

"Don't worry," I said. "You'll get it."

Monica promised to do the exercises and practice in front of a mirror.

Day 3

The next day, I had to watch Nick after school. So Monica came to my house. I kept Nick busy with a plate of cookies while Monica and I talked in the treehouse.

I had set up a few large pieces of poster board. They were *reminders* for Monica.

"What are those?" Monica asked.

"Cheerleader charts," I said. "To remind us what makes someone a good cheerleader."

Chart One: The Three Parts of Cheerleading

1. Gymnastics

2. Tumbling

3. Dance

Chart Two: The Four Cheer Groups

1. Movements

2. Jumps

3. Stunts

4. Chants

Chart Three: A Cheerleader Must Have:

1. Strength

2. Spirit

3. Smiles

"Stunts?" Monica asked nervously. "I can't do stunts."

Nick put down his plate of cookies. "I can. Watch!" he yelled. He did a somersault. He hit me with his feet.

"Let's go outside so Nick has more room," I suggested. The grass would be SOFTER and SAFER for Monica, too.

Nick went down the ladder first. He somersaulted across the lawn. Then he did a somersault backward.

"Can you do that?" he asked Monica. "Try this."
He did a handstand.

"I can flip, too," he told her.

I grabbed Nick's shirt. "Stop **showing off**, Nick," I
told him. "We're supposed to be training Monica."

"Can I help?" Nick asked. "Can I train Monica
too?"

Monica rolled her eyes. Then she shrugged.
"Sure," she said. Then she looked at me and
added, "But I still can't do STUNTS."

Monica looked **scared.** That was a good thing.
She wouldn't try anything **dangerous.** "We used to
do cartwheels," I reminded her.

Monica smiled and said, "Oh, yeah!" She took
a deep breath. She ran two steps and JUMPED.
She put one hand down and then the other.

Monica's arms and legs were supposed
to go up and over, like **spokes in a wheel.**
Instead, her legs were bent, not straight.
And they stuck out instead of up. She lost her
balance on the landing and **fell over.**

"That was awful!" Nick exclaimed.

"No, it wasn't," I said. I glared at him, but **Nick is glare-proof.**

"She looked like a **dizzy toad**," Nick said.

"Nick!" I snapped. "That's not nice."

"But it's true," Monica said quietly. "I can't be a cheerleader if I can't do stunts."

"Yes, you can," I said. "You take riding lessons. You know how to **pay attention** to what the horse is doing, what you're doing, and what the other riders are doing."

"So?" Monica asked. She looked puzzled.

"So you can be a **spotter**," I said.

"What's that?" Monica asked.

"Only some of the cheerleaders do the stunts," I explained. "They're called **flyers.** Then there are **bases.** Bases catch and hold the flyers. They need a **spotter** to count, watch the flyer, and help catch her. *You can do three things at once.*"

"That works!" Monica said, smiling. "I bet I can do a better cartwheel, too. I'll just have to work harder."

"I want more cookies," Nick said.

Day 4

On Saturday, I brought my dad's video camera to Monica's house.

Monica only had **two more days** to get ready. **I pushed harder.**

Here's what happened.

Monica: "Don't record me. I'll get nervous and mess up more."

Me: "You'll be nervous at the tryouts, too. This will help you get over it."

What I thought: The camera would show Monica her mistakes. Then she'd know what to fix.

Monica: "I'm sick of smiling. It's so fake."

Me: "You have to look happy, or you won't get picked."

What I thought: Nobody likes a cranky cheerleader.

Monica: "My legs hurt, and my arms feel like they're going to fall off. Even my face hurts."

Me: "Good! The exercises are working."

What I thought: You're the one who wanted this. Stop complaining!

Monica: "I am so tired! Can't we take a break?"

Me: "You have to cheer for a whole game. Ten more jumping jacks!"

What I thought: Losers rest. Winners work.

Monica: "Why are you being so mean, Claudia?"

Me: "Because Gina will be meaner."

What I thought: I hope we're still friends when this is over.

Day 5

I invited Monica to my house on Sunday.

"No practice today," I said. "Let's watch the video I made yesterday."

"But tryouts start tomorrow," Monica said. She sat down on the couch.

"That's why you should REST and RELAX," I explained.

I picked up the remote and sat down next to her.

"Wait for me!" Nick yelled, running into the room. He squeezed between Monica and me on the sofa. "Okay. **You can start now,**" he said.

I clicked PLAY.

Monica's stretching exercises looked good. Then she did a lunge.

It was hard to hold that position. Monica's smile twisted into a frown after a few seconds.

"Monica turned into a monster," Nick said.

Monica covered her eyes. "This is **awful**," she said.

"You have to watch," I said. "You need to pay attention, so you won't make the same mistakes at the tryouts."

Monica peeked through her fingers.

On the tape, Monica twirled. Her feet slipped out from under her. She squealed. Then she fell on the grass.

Nick laughed.

"It's like watching *America's Funniest Home Videos*," Monica said.

Nick laughed again. "Yeah!" he said. "Only you're **FUNNIER**."

"It's not that bad, Monica," I said. I was still watching the video. "Look! You did that jump **perfectly**."

"But my face is all **scrunched up**," Monica pointed out.

She sighed. "I'll never be a good cheerleader," she said. "I should quit before I make **a total fool** of myself."

"No way," I said.

Everyone at school already knew that Monica was planning to try out. It would be too **humiliating** if she quit now.

"Funny people are the **best part,**" Nick said.

"Of what?" Monica asked.

"Everything!" Nick exclaimed.

I shook my head and ignored Nick.

"You've worked **too hard** to give up,"
I told Monica. "And your cheers are getting
a lot better."

"Really?" Monica asked hopefully.

Nick and I both nodded.

"Just do your best," I said.

"And don't go like this,"
Nick added. He scrunched up his face.

CHAPTER 7

Jump Start

I wore a Pine Tree Middle School T-shirt on Monday. It has a picture of a big pine tree on the front. I taped a note to the tree. The note said: **Save Me!**

Everyone was too busy talking about cheerleading tryouts to notice my shirt.

"Are you NERVOUS, Monica?" **Adam** asked at lunch.

"A little," Monica admitted.

"That's okay," Peter said. *"Even rock stars get nervous before they go on stage."*

Tommy looked at me. He cocked his head and asked, "How many **straw wrappers** can you make from **one tree?**"

"I don't know," I admitted. I didn't have an answer. Someone had **finally** noticed the note on my shirt, and I didn't know what to say.

"Beats me," Becca said, shrugging.

"Thousands," Adam said. "Maybe even a million."

"Let's say it's A MILLION," Peter said. He found a pen in his backpack and started to scribble on his napkin. "Six kids times five days a week. We'd have to save our straw wrappers for 33,000 weeks to save one tree," Peter said.

"How many years is that?" Becca asked.

Peter scribbled more numbers.

"Six hundred and thirty-five," Peter said. "If I don't subtract vacation weeks."

Sometimes I wish that Peter wasn't so smart.

"Let's say we recycle straw wrappers until we graduate from high school," Tommy said. "We might save a twig." He held his hands two inches apart and added, "A twig about *this big*."

"Unless everyone at school recycles straw wrappers," I said. "Then it wouldn't take so long to save a whole tree."

"Okay! Okay!" **Adam** yelled. He threw up his hands. "I'll recycle my straw wrappers."

All my friends put their straw wrappers in the **recycling bin.** But I would have to remind them the next day, or they'd *forget* again.

My idea was starting to seem **pretty dumb.** I needed a greater cause. Something everybody really cared about. I couldn't think of anything.

* * *

Adam and I went to the cheerleading tryouts after school. Becca wouldn't go. She didn't want to watch Monica's hopes get crushed. She also didn't want to watch Monica become a snobby cool kid.

"Does Monica have a chance?" Adam asked me as we sat down in the bleachers.

I looked around the gym. Six girls were warming up. I was sure that Anna had made Carly and Karen practice, so her friends wouldn't mess up and look bad. Gina would definitely pick them.

That left Monica and two other girls, Kristin and Holly. One of them would be the fourth new cheerleader.

"She's got a one-in-three chance," I told Adam.

Adam shrugged. "That's not too bad," he said.

"Let's get started!" **Gina** yelled. "Everyone who's trying out, line up."

Adam gave Monica a **V for victory** sign. I smiled at her and waved. Then Monica started giggling.

"Oh no," I whispered. I'd forgotten that **Monica giggled when she was nervous!**

Monica took a deep breath. She stopped laughing, but she couldn't get rid of her GOOFY GRIN.

"Everyone follow me!" Gina yelled. She started doing some exercises.

The girls did jumping jacks, waist bends, and toe touches. Monica bent her knees a little during the toe touches. You're not supposed to do that. But she was the only one who smiled the whole time.

"This isn't a joke, Monica," Gina said.

"I know!" Monica exclaimed. She stopped smiling for one second. Then she giggled again and said, "I'm having fun! I love the Cougars! And **I love cheerleading!**"

"That's the spirit!" Gina said, grinning.

I stopped holding my breath.

Anna blinked with surprise. Then she  smiled too.

Next Gina showed the girls a basic cheer. She used two lunges and a spread eagle jump. She went over it three times. Then the new girls tried it.

"Pine Tree Middle is our school.

Go, Cougars! Go, Cougars!

Pine Tree Cougars rule!"

Monica's jump wasn't as high as Kristin's, and her split wasn't as wide as Linda's. She wobbled a little bit when she landed, but she kept smiling.

"Look straight ahead next time, Monica," Gina said. "That will help you keep your balance."

"Okay, thanks!" Monica said cheerfully.

Gina praised Anna, Carly, and Karen. She  frowned at **Kristin** and said, "You have to speak up. I couldn't hear you."

"Okay," Kristin whispered.

She stared at the floor. I wondered why Kristin wanted to be a cheerleader. She was **a math genius**. She wasn't quite as smart as Peter, but she was just as shy.

Then Gina looked at Holly. "Your cheer was okay, but the jump wasn't high enough," **Gina** said.

Holly nodded. "Jump higher. Got it," she said.

Gina taught the girls two more cheers. Monica forgot some words and missed a couple moves, but she smiled the whole time. *I thought she did a good job.*

Kristin and Holly got the cheers right. Kristin shouted louder, smiled, and started looking up. Holly jumped higher.

Gina ignored them. She loved Anna and her friends.

And she loved Monica.

CHAPTER 8

Cheerleader Dares

In homeroom the next morning, everyone stopped talking when Anna and Carly walked in.

I didn't want to say it looked like **a freak show.** But it looked like a freak show.

"What's going on?" Becca asked.

"I think we're asleep," Adam said. "In **Anna's nightmare.**"

"Maybe Anna turned colorblind overnight," Becca said.

"Or she wants to be **a clown** when she grows up," **Tommy** joked.

I didn't laugh. Something was weird.

Anna loves clothes. She pays attention to all the fashion trends and only wears cool clothes. **Her outfits always match.**

But today, Anna was wearing a top with red and white stripes, a green skirt, and purple socks. *Her sneakers had holes in the toes.* She looked really strange. Her outfit didn't match at all.

"You guys, look at Carly's hair," Becca whispered. We all turned to look.

Carly's hair was SPIKED with gel. The spikes were colored yellow, red, and green. They stood up all over her head. She looked like **an exploding beach ball.**

"It's just Cheerleader Dare Day," Jenny Pinski said.

"What's Cheerleader Dare Day?" I asked.

"The girls on the cheerleading squad dare the girls trying out," Jenny explained. "They have to do something **embarrassing.** To prove how much they want to be cheerleaders."

Adam, Becca, and I turned to look at Monica. **Monica pretended she didn't notice.**

Then the bell rang.

* * *

Becca and I have first period math with Mr. Chen.

Kristin is in our class too. Kristin wasn't wearing weird clothes. Everything seemed normal. Mr. Chen asked a question, and Kristin raised her hand to answer it. She was *a math whiz* and always knew the answers. But she said, **"I don't know."**

That was weird!

Kristin did the same thing later that morning in history.

Becca stopped her after class. "Are you doing a cheerleader dare, Kristin?" Becca asked.

"I don't know," Kristin said.

Just then, another cheerleader walked by. "Does two plus two equal four?" the cheerleader asked.

"I don't know," Kristin said.

The cheerleader laughed and kept walking.

Becca and I followed Kristin to the cafeteria. "I wonder what Monica has to do," I said quietly.

"I think we're about to find out," Becca said. She pointed into the cafeteria.

I looked at our table. **Monica** was standing on a chair. She held up one hand. Her other hand was on her hip.

"I'm a little teapot, short and stout," Monica sang. She did all the little kid motions that went with the song. We learned it in **kindergarten.** Monica sang the whole thing.

"What are we going to do?" Becca asked.

"Tell her the truth," I said.

A Real Friend

. . . *tells a friend when she's making a mistake, even if it makes her mad.*

Anna and Carly ran over to Monica before Becca and I got there.

"Tryouts will be over Friday," **Anna** told Monica. "**It'll be worth it** when we make the squad."

"See you later," Carly said. She smiled and waved as they walked away.

Monica's face was SWEATY. She smiled and waved at Carly and Anna.

Becca and I sat down at the table with Monica.

"Was that your cheerleader dare?" I asked.

Monica nodded. She **blushed with embarrassment.**

"Why did Gina make you do that?" Becca asked. "Isn't being a good cheerleader enough?"

"It should be enough," I said.

Monica poked at her **fries** with her fork.

"It's pretty stupid to do stuff so the eighth graders think you're cool," I said.

"You're just jealous because the popular kids like me now," Monica said. "Gina said I have a good chance to make the squad. I don't need your help anymore, Claudia."

"Okay," I said quietly. I didn't ask if we were still best friends. **I wasn't sure I'd like the answer.**

CHAPTER 9

Greater Cause

I didn't sleep well that night. I was too upset about Monica. But I wasn't tired when I got up the next morning.

I was really **WORRIED**. I might lose my best friend. But now I had found **a greater cause than recycling straw wrappers.**

At lunch, I stood on a chair. Everybody stared at me. Maybe they thought I was going to sing another **kindergarten song**, like Monica had the day before.

"I think we should change how Pine Tree Middle School picks cheerleaders," I said loudly.

Everyone groaned and went back to their lunches. I kept going anyway. "A group of students and teachers would pick **the best cheerleaders**," I said. "We shouldn't just keep picking the most popular kids. Unless they're **the best**, of course."

I didn't mention cheerleader dares. The dares would stop if the older girls didn't pick the new girls.

"That's all," I said. Then I sat down.

Nobody clapped. **My announcement was a flop.**

Monica leaned over and glared at me. "You don't want me to make the squad," she said quietly. Her eyes flashed. She was *really mad.*

"Yes I do," I said. "That's why I helped you practice all last week."

"Gina likes me," Monica said. "I was going to make the squad. But now you want to **change the rules.**" Monica picked up her tray and left.

Anna and Carly waved her over. Monica sat down with them. They were glad to see her.

I felt awful. We were having **macaroni and cheese with brownies for dessert.** It was my favorite school lunch, but I wasn't hungry anymore.

"The eighth-grade cheerleaders have always picked the new cheerleaders," **Adam** said.

"But the tryouts should be fair," I said.

Becca sighed. "Will Monica ever be our friend again?" she asked.

"Sure," I said. "When she stops being mad."

I've known Monica since kindergarten. I didn't believe she'd pick cheerleading and Anna over Becca and me. For one thing, Monica always plays fair. She just wasn't thinking straight. 𝓡𝓘𝓖𝓗𝓣?

Anna came over to our table. She put her hands on her hips. "The popular girls have always been cheerleaders, Claudia," she told me. "It's a tradition. **You can't change tradition.**"

"I can try," I said.

I wasn't as sure as I sounded. **I knew that people didn't like change.** Not even if change was going to make things better.

My great cause might be another lost cause.

Like **saving a tree.**

I didn't tell my friends to recycle their straw wrappers, so they all forgot. I recycled mine before I dumped my tray.

I could save a tree by myself. It would only take **three thousand years.**

"Oops!" said **Adam.** He pulled his straw wrapper out of the trashcan. Then he put it in the recycling bin and smiled at me.

I smiled back. "Thanks," I told him. It wasn't a big thing, but it made me feel better. Adam recycled because he saw me do it.

Too bad **leading by example** wouldn't help me change how Pine Tree Middle School chose cheerleaders.

CHAPTER 10

Who Cares?

After school, I stopped at Mr. Gomez's house. He lives across the street from me with Mrs. Gomez and her poodle. **Mr. Gomez treats me like an adult.** He listens when I talk, and he always has good advice.

"How's the cheerleading practice going?" Mr. Gomez asked.

"Monica's working with the squad now," I said. I didn't want to talk about Monica. So I asked, "How do you get people to change something they don't want to change?"

Mr. Gomez scratched his head. Then he rubbed his chin. "Why don't they want to change it?" he asked.

"Because it's always been done one way," I said.

"Ah, I see," Mr. Gomez said, nodding. "It's a TRADITION."

"But the tradition isn't FAIR," I said. "There's got to be a better way."

"Maybe people don't know that," Mr. Gomez said. "Maybe they've never really thought about it. So get their attention. **Make them think about it.**"

"Thanks, Mr. Gomez," I said. "That's good advice."

But I wasn't sure how to make anyone think about cheerleading tryouts.

At home, Mom was in the kitchen baking cookies. I didn't see Nick, so I sat down.

"How do you get ATTENTION for a good cause?" I asked.

"Well, when I worked for a charity in college, we made telephone calls," Mom said.

I loved talking on the phone, but I couldn't call every kid in school.

"TV and newspaper interviews help," Mom went on.

I thought about that. An article in the school newspaper would help, but the editor of the *Pinecone Press* wouldn't print an article if he liked the way **cheerleaders were picked now.**

"Sometimes we asked people to sign a **petition**," Mom said. "That works really well."

"It does? Why?" I asked.

"People ask what the petition is about," **Mom** said. "Then you can explain *why* they should support your cause."

PERFECT!

* * *

My petition looked great. My brother, **Jimmy,** designed it on his computer. He printed out 20 copies. Each page had lines for 20 signatures.

20 signatures x 20 pages = 400

There were **500** students at Pine Tree Middle School. I probably wouldn't get **400** signatures. But my dad always says, **"Think big, Claudia!"**

I was pretty sure Coach Campbell and Principal Paul would listen if 100 people signed the petition. That was my goal.

I went to school the next day prepared to push my cause.

I put the petition pages on a clipboard. I carried a pen. I also wore my **tree t-shirt** with the "Save Me!" note. Someone might ask about it. Maybe I could change how cheerleaders are picked and **save a tree** too!

I stood outside the main doors. Larry Kyle was the first kid to walk by. "Do you want to sign my petition?" I asked.

Larry noticed my shirt. "What are you trying to save?" he asked.

"A tree," I said. "If I recycle my straw wrappers at lunch, it will take **three thousand years.**"

"To save one tree?" Larry asked. "So it would take 10 kids 300 years or 100 kids 30 years. 500 Pine Tree Middle School kids could save a tree in 6 years!"

"Exactly!" I said, smiling.

"Even quicker if we recycle **homework** and **test papers,** too. Where's the pen?" Larry asked, reaching out. "I'll sign."

"My petition isn't about that," I said. "It's about trying to make **cheerleader tryouts** more fair."

"Oh," Larry said. He shrugged. "No thanks."

For the next fifteen minutes, I asked everyone I saw to sign my petition.

Everyone had a reason why they wouldn't sign.

Reasons

1. "I don't want to make Gina mad."

2. "I don't want to make Anna mad."

3. "I don't want to be the only one to sign the petition."

When the bell rang, I only had **four** signatures.

CHAPTER 11

The Biggest Dare

The next day, **more bad stuff than good stuff** happened.

In the morning, ten sixth graders signed my petition. Adam, Tommy, Peter, and Becca signed it too, but mostly so that I'd stop asking.

Before lunch, I saw **Brad Turino** in the hallway. I knew I had to ask him to sign the petition. I'd regret it if I didn't.

I talked fast so I wouldn't get **tongue-tied.** "Will you sign my petition to make picking cheerleaders more fair?" I asked.

"Sure!" Brad said. He smiled. "That's just good sportsmanship," he added.

That's why Brad is the love of my life. He's cute, cool, and totally not conceited or selfish.

Then I had a total of 19 signers. I only needed 81 more to reach **100**.

At lunch, **Monica** wouldn't talk to me. She talked to Becca a little. But she sat with Anna and Carly.

All my friends recycled their straw wrappers. Adam reminded them. That was TERRIFIC.

After school, I saw Monica walk into the locker room. It was time for her last practice before the final tryouts the next day.

I went outside and waited for Becca on the sidewalk. After a few minutes, she ran out the doors. She was breathless when she reached me.

"I've got something **terrible** to tell you," **Becca** said. She sat down on the grass to catch her breath. Then she added, "It's about Monica."

"What's the matter with Monica?" I asked.

"I'm not exactly sure," Becca said. "This morning she told me that she wouldn't be going through all this if she didn't have a chance to make the squad."

"Going through all what stuff?" I asked. "Practice? **Keeping her hair combed?** Smiling at everyone except us? Being nice to Anna?"

"I thought Monica meant practice," Becca said. "Then I heard her talking to Kristin about **the final test.**"

"She was probably talking about the tryouts," I said.

At the tryouts, the new girls had to perform cheers. So **tryouts** were like a **test.**

It didn't really mean anything. **Gina** had already decided who would make the squad.

"I don't think so," Becca said quietly. She frowned and added, "They said they could get **suspended** if they got caught!"

* * *

Monica can be *ultra-super-unbelievably stubborn.* When she makes up her mind, she's like **gum stuck on a shoe.** Nothing can get it off. Nothing can ever change her mind.

Monica was **determined** to be a cheerleader. She might even do something awful because Gina told her to.

So when we got to my house, Becca and I called Monica. Becca told Monica that it was IMPORTANT.

After cheerleading practice, Monica showed up in the treehouse in my back yard. I could tell that she thought we wanted to apologize and wish her **good luck** at tryouts.

"What do you have to do to be picked?" Becca asked.

Monica told us the things she had to remember for tryouts.

Monica's Tryout Reminders

1. Smile and relax

2. Be peppy and enthusiastic

3. Keep hair off face

4. Use a loud, clear voice

5. Keep going if you make a mistake

6. Look like you're having a good time even if you're totally tired, nervous, and stressed out.

"That's not what Becca meant," I said. "We're worried about the big dare."

"What big dare?" Monica asked.

She tried to look **innocent,** but she was tapping her foot and nibbling her lip. She always did that when she felt GUILTY.

"The one that could get you **suspended,**" Becca said. "What did Gina ask you to do?"

Monica sighed. She looked down at the ground.

"We have to put *vegetable oil* on classroom doorknobs so they'll be slippery," she told us. "Then no one will be able to go to class."

"Can't they just **wipe it off?**" Becca asked.

Monica shrugged. "I guess," she said.

"What if a teacher sees you?" I asked.

"Why do you care?" Monica snapped. *She glared at me.*

I knew she wasn't really mad. Sometimes people act mad when they know they're wrong.

"We're your friends, Monica," I said. "We don't want you to get in trouble."

A Real Friend

. . . tells a friend when she's making a mistake,

even if it makes her mad.

Sooner or later she'll get over it.

"I have to go," Monica said. She stood up and headed out the treehouse door.

Becca started to follow Monica, but I grabbed her arm.

"We have to **trust** Monica to do the right thing," I explained. Monica had to figure out the right thing to do.

CHAPTER 12

Sun-up Showdown

"Sometimes big change happens one small step at a time," my mom once told me.

I tried to remember that, so I wouldn't feel FRUSTRATED.

But all of my steps were so small! I'd be an **old lady** before Pine Tree Middle School had fair cheerleader tryouts.

But great leaders don't give up.

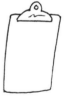

Later that night, I called Becca. I told her my plan. She agreed to help.

Friday morning we met on the corner. I gave Becca a petition clipboard and a pen.

We walked to school early, but **the cheerleaders had gotten there first.**

Becca and I hid behind a tree and watched. Monica was standing on the steps with a bottle of vegetable oil and a rag.

The other seventh graders had oil and rags, too.

Nobody looked happy. Not even Anna and Carly.

Gina and the other eighth-grade cheerleaders weren't there. I guess they didn't want to be around if the younger girls got caught.

Becca was SHOCKED. "I can't believe Monica's going to grease doorknobs!" she whispered.

"She hasn't done anything yet," I said.

Monica waved her rag. "I've got something to say," she told the other cheerleaders.

The other girls looked at her.

"We've practiced all week to learn the Cougar cheers," Monica said. "We've worked hard to be **cheerleaders,** not *criminals!*"

All the girls were quiet for a second.

Then Linda yelled, "That's right!"

"So I'm not going to do Gina's **stupid dare,**" Monica said. She marched down the steps and dropped her oil and rag in a garbage can.

"I'm not going to either," **Kristin** said. She threw away her oil and rag.

Then Linda and Karen threw theirs away too.

Anna and Carly hesitated.

"If you don't oil doorknobs," **Anna** said, "Gina won't pick you for the squad."

"She'll have to pick **two** of us," Monica said. "The squad needs four new cheerleaders."

"Yeah, and you can't be a cheerleader if you get **suspended**," Kristin pointed out.

Anna and Carly looked at each other. Then they tossed their oil and rags too.

All of the girls grinned and gave each other high fives.

"And one more thing!" Monica yelled to get everyone's attention. "The **best cheerleaders** should be on the squad, like Claudia said. Not the most POPULAR kids."

"That's not going to happen," Anna said.

"It WILL happen if we want it to," Monica said.

She pointed at the tree where Becca and I were hiding. "I'll sign your petition, Claudia," she called.

I smiled. Then I walked over to Monica and handed her **my clipboard.** Kristin and Linda signed too.

"That was so cool, Monica!" I said, smiling. "You're turning out to be **a great leader,** just like you wanted to be."

"I am?" Monica asked. She looked SURPRISED.

"Absolutely!" I exclaimed. "You stood up for what's right. Against Gina! Even though it might ruin your chance to be a cheerleader."

"She's right," Becca said.

"I guess I did," **Monica** said.

"And you stopped all those other girls from making **a huge mistake,**" I pointed out. "Everyone followed your lead. Even Anna."

"Then you're a great leader too, Claudia," Monica said, smiling. **"You inspired me."**

"Does that mean we're friends again?" I asked.

"Always," Monica said. "Even when we get mad. No matter what. **Friends Forever.**"

CHAPTER 13

P.S.

After Monica and the other girls signed the petition, two hundred other kids signed too. So Coach Campbell and Principal Paul changed how cheerleaders are chosen. **Starting this year.**

Coach Campbell, Principal Paul, Gina, and one student from each grade picked the new cheerleaders. The girls were judged on **performance** and **ATTITUDE.** It turned out that all of the girls who tried out made the squad. The judges said **everyone** deserved it.

Monica decided that she didn't want to be a cheerleader after all. She'd rather spend her time with her **friends** and **horses.** She decided not to try out.

My friends started telling other kids at school to **recycle paper.** Now everyone is doing it. Teachers are recycling test and homework papers, too. **We'll probably save a tree every year!**

And Nick is still driving me crazy. Some things never change.

About the Author

Diana G. Gallagher lives in Florida with her husband and five dogs, four cats, and a cranky parrot. Her hobbies are gardening, garage sales, and grandchildren. She has been an English equitation instructor, a professional folk musician, and an artist. However, she had aspirations to be a professional writer at the age of twelve. She has written dozens of books for kids and young adults.

About the Illustrator

Brann Garvey lives in Minneapolis, Minnesota with his wife, Keegan, and their very fat cat, Iggy. Brann graduated from Iowa State University with a bachelor of fine arts degree. He later attended the Minneapolis College of Art and Design, where he studied illustration. In his free time, Brann enjoys being with his family and friends. He brings his sketchbook everywhere he goes.

Glossary

causes (KAWZ-iz)—aims or principles for which people fight, raise money, etc.

conceited (kuhn-SEE-tid)—if you are conceited, you are too proud of yourself and of what you can do

consequences (KON-suh-kwenss-iz)—results of actions

enthusiasm (en-THOO-zee-az-uhm)—great excitement or interest

frustrated (FRUHSS-tray-tid)—if you are frustrated, you feel helpless or discouraged

impulsive (im-PUHL-sive)—an impulsive person acts without thinking first

petition (puh-TISH-uhn)—a letter signed by many people that tells those in power how the signers feel about an issue or situation

signature (SIG-nuh-chur)—the individual way that a person writes his or her name

tradition (truh-DISH-uhn)—an idea, belief, or activity that is always performed the same way

tryouts (TRYE-outs)—a trial or test to see if a person is able to do something

Discussion Questions

1. How are sports teams and cheerleading squads chosen in your school? Do you think it is a fair method? Why or why not?

2. What is the right thing to do when a friend does something you don't agree with? Do you think Claudia did the right thing?

3. Does your school recycle? If so, do you think the recycling program is good or bad? If your school doesn't recycle, do you think it should?

Writing Prompts

1. In this book, Claudia wants to be a good leader. Write about a time that you were a good leader. What happened? How did you prove that you were a good leader?

2. Have you ever had a fight with one of your best friends? What was the fight about? How was it resolved?

3. Claudia thinks that the way cheerleaders are picked is unfair. Write about something you think is unfair. What is it? Why isn't it fair? How could it be made more fair?

MORE FUN
with Claudia!

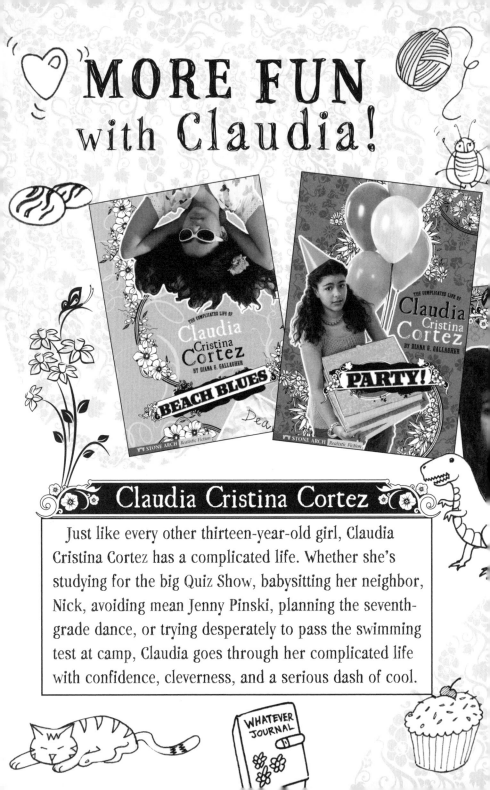

THE COMPLICATED LIFE OF
Claudia Cristina Cortez
BY DIANA G. GALLAGHER
BEACH BLUES

THE COMPLICATED LIFE OF
Claudia Cristina Cortez
BY DIANA G. GALLAGHER
PARTY!

❀ Claudia Cristina Cortez ❀

Just like every other thirteen-year-old girl, Claudia Cristina Cortez has a complicated life. Whether she's studying for the big Quiz Show, babysitting her neighbor, Nick, avoiding mean Jenny Pinski, planning the seventh-grade dance, or trying desperately to pass the swimming test at camp, Claudia goes through her complicated life with confidence, cleverness, and a serious dash of cool.

WHATEVER JOURNAL

David Mortimore Baxter

David is a great kid, but he has one big problem — he can't stop talking. These wildly humorous stories, told by David himself, will show you just how much trouble a boy and his mouth can get into, whether he's making promises to become class president or bragging that he's best friends with the world's most famous wrestler. David is fun, engaging, cool, and smart enough to realize that growing up is the biggest adventure of all.

Internet Sites

Do you want to know more about subjects related to this book? Or are you interested in learning about other topics? Then check out FactHound, a fun, easy way to find Internet sites.

Our investigative staff has already sniffed out great sites for you!

Here's how to use FactHound:

1. Visit *www.facthound.com*

2. Select your grade level.

3. To learn more about subjects related to this book, type in the book's ISBN number: **9781434207722**.

4. Click the **Fetch It** button.

FactHound will fetch the best Internet sites for you!